MANDA HANSON studied calligraphy, heraldry (the art of tracing genealogies and designing coats of arms) and illumination at Reigate School of Art. Now a freelancer, Manda has undertaken many commissions including some for the College of Arms. She has taught part-time in adult education since leaving College in 1985, and now mainly does commercial art.

COLOR
Calligraphy
Projects

WORKSTATION

WORKSTATION *is a new concept comprising all the*
elements you need to begin the art of decorative calligraphy.

Within the first 48 pages are alphabets and projects
illustrated using the pen, brush, and paints supplied in this kit.
An additional 16 pages including colored paper, grids, a stencil,
and two alphabets to be used with the various projects are
supplied at the back of the book for practice work.
Eleven distinctly lovely projects can be created in
COLOR CALLIGRAPHY PROJECTS WORKSTATION.

Manda Hanson

PRICE STERN SLOAN
Los Angeles

A PRICE STERN SLOAN—DESIGN EYE BOOK

Line illustrations by Adrian Deadman
© 1993 Design Eye Holdings Ltd.
Produced by Design Eye Holdings Ltd.
First published in the United States by Price Stern Sloan, Inc.,
A member of The Putnam & Grosset Group, New York, New York.

ISBN: 0-8431-3759-2
First Edition
1 3 5 7 9 10 8 6 4 2

Printed in China by Giftech Ltd.

Warning:
This product is intended as a beginner's guide for ages 8 and up.
Contains a functional sharp point.
Children under 8 years of age should be strictly supervised by an adult.
Conforms to ASTM D 4236-92

CONTENTS

INTRODUCTION

*C*ALLIGRAPHY COMES FROM THE GREEK *Kallos graphe, meaning beautiful handwriting. The aim of this book is to combine beautiful handwriting with other techniques to produce some interesting and colorful projects.*

Each chapter introduces you to a calligraphic alphabet. Once you have mastered this, you will then be taken through several stages to a finished project. Following the alphabets and the projects step-by-step will give you a good basis for later developing your own ideas.

Most of the materials you need are provided in the workstation. There are, however, a few additional items that you will need to get yourself, such as the T-shirt and some thick card for the 18th and 21st birthday cards. The finished projects in the workstation have all been carried out using the materials provided.

This is a Celtic 'P.' It is the Lord's Prayer written out in Latin. The P itself is 23 ¼ carat gold leaf, with a raised center pattern. The background is diffused and stained with tea to give an old, antique look to the work.

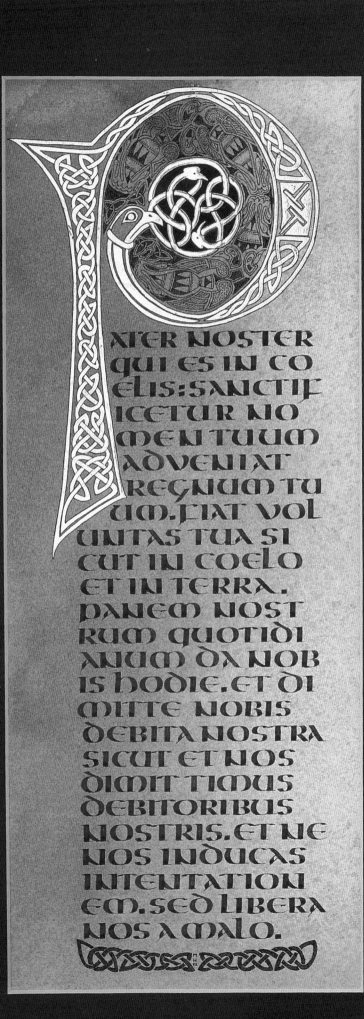

PATER NOSTER
QUI ES IN CO
ELIS: SANCTIF
ICETUR NO
MEN TUUM
ADVENIXT
REGNUM TU
UM. FIXT VOL
UNTAS TUA SI
CUT IN COELO
ET IN TERRA.
PANEM NOST
RUM QUOTIDI
ANUM DA NOB
IS HODIE. ET DI
MITTE NOBIS
DEBITA NOSTRA
SICUT ET NOS
DIMIT TIMUS
DEBITORIBUS
NOSTRIS. ET NE
NOS INDUCAS
INTENTATION
EM. SED LIBERA
NOS A MALO.

DECORATING
WITH ITALIC

THE ITALIC HAND IS A quickly written alphabet developed in Italy during the Renaissance. It is a very elegant hand which, once you have mastered it, will enable you to achieve some beautiful results. I find it the most useful of the various alphabets and I use it more than any other hand. It is easy to read and ideal for projects like birthday cards. It is as well to remember when sending cards that the recipient may not be as familiar with calligraphic shapes as you are, so a simple, flowing alphabet such as italic is often an ideal choice to use.

In this first project, you will learn a basic italic hand, you will then learn many different ways of decorating it and, finally, you will be shown how to use it on cards.

PROJECT 1

In order to follow the alphabet, begin at the dot then note the arrows and numbers, which indicate the direction and order of strokes.

To start with, we will practice some flow exercises. Using the pen provided and the grid at the back of the book, mix up the paint in a saucer. Squeeze approximately $\frac{1}{4}$ inch of paint from the tube and mix this with about six drops of water. Make sure that the reservoir fits snuggly on the nib. The reservoir should be about $\frac{1}{16}$ inch below the end of the nib and should just touch the back of the nib. The reservoir controls the flow of paint through the slit in the nib. When you fill the nib, use the brush provided in the workstation and brush the paint over the reservoir.

Getting the paint to flow can be quite frustrating. It depends on many conditions being right.

• The paint should be of a good consistency similar to that of milk. If it is too thick, it will not flow out of the the nib, and if it is too thin, the lettering will appear patchy and may blob.

thick, blobby paint

watery paint

• Check that the reservoir fits properly and is just touching the back of the nib.

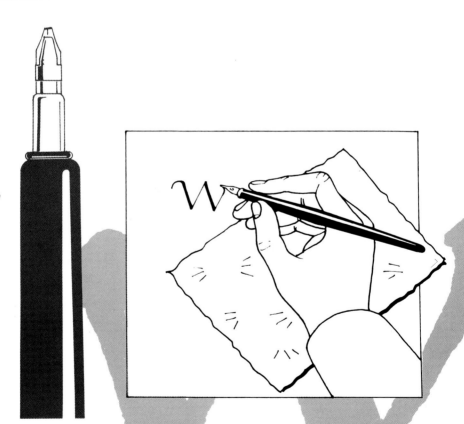

• Make sure the surface you are writing on is clean and free from grease. Try to have a piece of paper under your hand at all times, however clean your hands are, as grease or sweat may rub off onto the paper and make it almost impossible to write on.

FLOW EXERCISES

Use the flow exercises as a means to get the pen working efficiently. Only attempt the letters once you are confident that everything is working properly for you.

FLOW EXERCISES – do not lift the pen off the paper

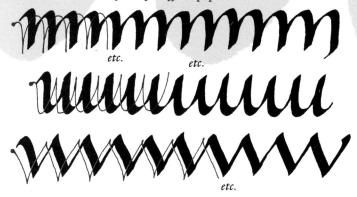

etc.   *etc.*

etc.

TERMINOLOGY

ASCENDER HEIGHT
(does not have to be strictly adhered to)
CAPITAL HEIGHT
LOWER CASE HEIGHT *or* TOP LINE

X HEIGHT

BASE LINE

DESCENDER LENGTH *(again, for this italic, it does not have to be strictly adhered to)*

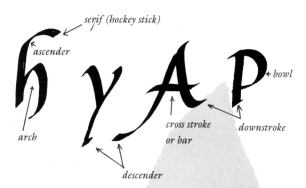

serif (hockey stick)

ascender

bowl

arch

cross stroke
or bar

downstroke

descender

When you start the alphabet, remember to keep the pen at an angle of about 40–45 degrees.

angle too sharp, letter appears too skinny	*angle too shallow, letter appears heavy*	*correct angle 40–45°*

This alphabet is based on a nice oval "O," so practice this letter first.

oooooooooo

Practice the other letters in these groups. Note that the height of this lower case italic is 4 nib widths (use the grid provided at the back of the workstation).

Try these few words as a spacing exercise.

ceo   bp   adgq

vwxy

hmnurt

fijklsz

illumination

minimum

The capital alphabet is 6 nib widths high (2 nib widths higher than the lower case).

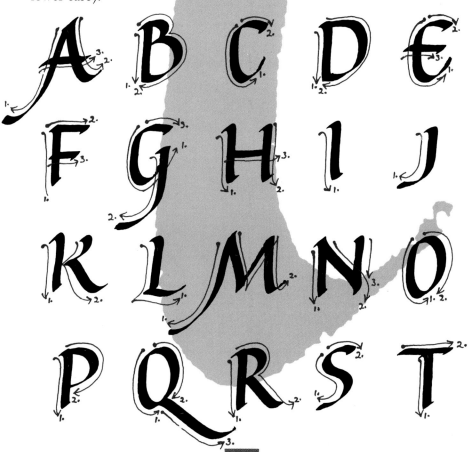

The numbers illustrated here can be used with the Italic alphabet included in the Workstation.

One basic rule when trying to achieve good spacing is to remember that two straight strokes end up farther apart than a straight stroke and a curve, and two curves are even closer.

Two straight strokes end up farther apart

A straight stroke and a curve are closer

Two curves are even closer

If you find that your writing tends to lean, don't worry; it is permissible to do this with the italic hand, provided that all the letters lean in the same direction! On the other hand do not force your writing to lean, as you will find the lettering will not flow well and do not allow it to lean backward.

may lean forward

but not backward

can also be upright

SHADOW ITALIC

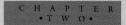

PROJECT 2

WITH THIS FORM OF DECORATION, the aim is to achieve a shadow effect. While you are practicing this, it is a good idea to imagine that the lettering is three-dimensional and there is a light source coming from the top left-hand corner.

light source

In this way, it is easier to see where the shadows will fall.

USING THE MAPPING PEN

The idea is to make the lines of the shadow using the mapping nib (this does not require the reservoir). Place the nib into the pen handle then you can either paint the color on top of the nib or you can dip the nib in the paint in order to fill the letter. Be careful not to overload the pen, otherwise it may blob. By putting slight pressure on the nib, the paint will flow down the split and produce a fine line. Again, practice on a piece of rough paper, making sure the paint is of the right consistency. When you use the gold color, it will be neccessary to stir it frequently as it tends to separate more than any of the other paints.

a b c d e f g h

i j k l m n o p

q r s t u v w

x y z A B C

D E F G H I J

K L M N O P

Q R S T U V

W X Y Y Z

To decorate these letters further you can add some dots halfway up the stem of the letter. It is advisable to draw a very light pencil line where you want the dots to fall, so that they appear even.

Happy Birthday

The pencil line can then be rubbed out when the paint has completely dried.

Greetings

Thankyou

Note the different descenders used for the G's.

Flourishes are an extension of the letter and should not alter the shape of the letter in any way. Draw a pencil line as a guide.

You can also reverse the shadow effect so it becomes a highlight.

Reversed Shadow Effect

14

The shadow and dot decoration is good to use when you are doing only one or two words. It is not practical to use it with a whole block of text or several verses of a poem. It can be used however to decorate the title so that it stands out well.

Now try experimenting with the colors provided in the workstation. White can be added to any of the colors, red and blue can be mixed to make purple, and so on. Different-colored cards can also produce good results when white or gold paint is used.

DESIGNING A THANK-YOU CARD

PROJECT 3

TEAR THE PIECE OF CREAM card out of the back of the book and fold in half widthways.

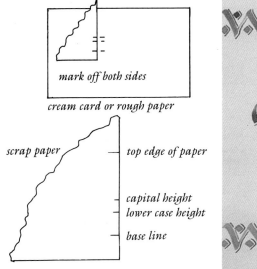

mark off both sides

cream card or rough paper

scrap paper — *top edge of paper*

capital height
lower case height

base line

1. Then, on a piece of rough paper, write out the words *Thank you*. You will need to draw a base line, a top line, and a capital height line to enable you to get the lettering even.

2. Practice the words, *Thank you* until you feel they are evenly spaced and will fit on the card.

3. Use the grid, and transfer the writing lines onto the scrap paper, then onto the rough paper, and finally onto your cream card.

Remember that there should be slightly more room below the words *Thank you* than above them. For a more decorative effect you can extend the "*Th*" to join and extend the letter "*Y*." Decide on the colors you want to use, write out the words and decorate them. A strip of pattern (derived from the flow exercises) can be drawn above and below the *Thank you,* transferring measurements in the same way as *Thank you.*

PROJECT 4

Using the decorations already discussed as well as a few others, here are some ideas for card designs, for using inside cards, for bookmarks and just for decorating the italic alphabet.

Flourishes can used to their fullest with italic. There are just three points to remember:

Badly executed flourish

This is correct. The form of the letter is still clearly visible.

1. All flourishes form the letters must appear as extensions of the letters, and must not in any way change their shape or form.

Nice and strong and elegant, curved only at the ends, subtle

Too wavy, appears weak

2. Line flourishes must be kept straight and curved only toward the end.

3. Remember to have plenty of paint on your pen so that you don't have to stop halfway through a flourish; this would make it disjointed.

Congratulations

happy 18th

Get Well
S·O·O·N

Keep to only 1 or 2 colors and perhaps gold.
Too many colors can start to look messy.

Happy
Anniversary

Best Wishes

WELL DONE
you passed

Just a few letters with some decoration and color added can make an interesting design.

CON
GRAT
U
LA
TIONS

Thank
you

Where one word is centered upon another word it will be necessary to practice writing these out. Nothing looks worse than badly centered lettering.

Fill only a few letters with a block of color, otherwise the words can be hard to read.

HAPPY
21st

Good
Luck

Merry Christmas

Pencil in these flourishes first, making sure they form a nice balanced design.

SEASONS

GREETINGS

Happy New Year

NOEL
NOEL
NOEL

HAPPY
X·MAS

These bookmark designs have been freely written out (no lines) and the decoration added last.

You may need to write out the letters several times before you have a satisfactory design—a good way to practice, anyway!

ITALIC CURSIVE

These sampler alphabets have been written out in white on a rough, textured background. A little gold has been added just for interest.

Again use flourishes carefully on the letters. Make sure you can still tell what the letters are!

ITALIC   CURSIVE

21ST AND 18TH BIRTHDAY CARDS

PROJECT 5

FOR THIS PROJECT, YOU WILL need to provide:
• a piece of thin, colored card 6 inches wide by 7 ³/₄ inches high when folded • a craft knife • some tracing paper

Trace the number you need from the back of the workstation. Then using a softer pencil, such as a 2B, trace over the back of your tracing.

Now place the tracing the right way up onto your folded card. Make sure the "*1*" of the number "*18*" is placed to the fold and the "*2*" of the number "*21*" is also placed to the fold.

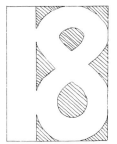
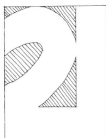

Use a slightly harder pencil, such as an HB, to draw over the tracing. Do not exert too much pressure, though, as you may indent the card and be left with an unsightly line.

Remove the tracing paper and use a ruler to re-draw the straight lines, re-draw over the number if you find your lines are too faint. Now very carefully using a craft knife remove all the sections masked with shading. Do not cut the fold.

Now trace the baseline, topline and capital height line from the "*21*" and "*18*" at the base of the workstation.

Writing on a curve needs practice and patience!

It would be helpful to practice writing on a curve before embarking on the finished piece. It is quite different to writing on a straight line—the paper must be continually moved so each letter becomes upright and does not look like it's at a funny angle.

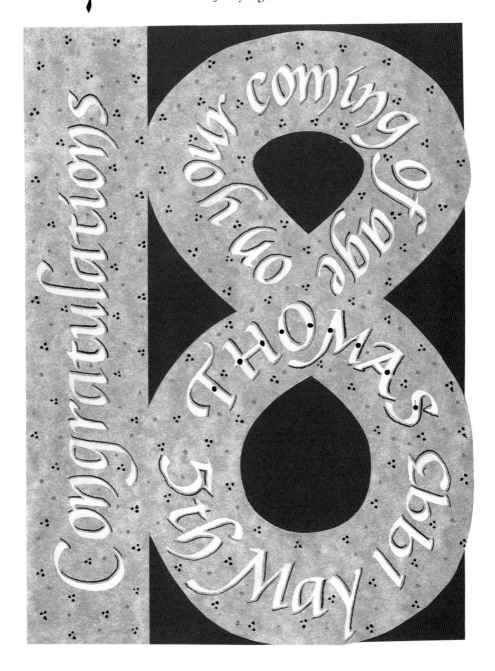

Now practice writing on a curve. When you use pale colors on dark card, it may be neccessary to use the paint slightly thicker than usual, but it must still be fluid enough to flow in the pen. Write out the name, date, and message in pencil first, then in paint.

You can then either shadow the lettering or use feathery foliage. For the 21st card, lightly pencil in the foliage, go over it with green paint and add some pink and gold dots, using the mapping nib.

For both the cards, you could insert a contrasting colored piece of card on which to write your own special message.

An Illuminated Initial

PROJECT 6

ILLUMINATION IS THE USE OF gold, usually combined with colored inks or paints to give a jewel-like effect. The letters we are using are taken from various Augsburg Presses, during the period 1473–1482. They were printed and either left as an outline or hand-colored. We will be applying color and gold to our letters. Unfortunately, not all the letters were provided but by using parts of some of the letters, it has been possible to complete the alphabet.

For this project you will need:
• *tracing paper* • *HB pencil* • *2B pencil* • *a saucer or paint palette*

Using the HB pencil, trace the letter of your choice, including the border, and re-draw the letter on the back with the 2B pencil. Now place the letter centrally on the cream paper found in the back of the workstation (it can be folded and used as a card, or cut in two and used for two letters).

Using the HB pencil, trace the letter down, being careful not to press too hard as you don't want to indent the paper. The tracing can be held down with paper clips, or with tape that is not too sticky (to avoid ripping the surface of the paper). Remove the tracing paper and re-draw the lines if they are not clear enough. It is important at this point that you are clear about the floral decoration and where each strand goes under or over another branch.

The first stage is to lay down all the gold. Mix the gold to the same consistency as the colored paint. Outline the shape to be filled in with gold and, using the mapping pen, flood the gold paint onto the area: Pull the paint across to the cover the area, making sure the mapping nib has plenty of paint on it. Apply just enough pressure to slit the nib, so that the paint flows down and floods the outline of gold. Very large areas should be filled in with a brush, but the areas on these letters are small enough and only require the mapping nib.

To draw a straight line, use a ruler with a bevel, placed upside-down on the paper and using the mapping pen draw across the edge of the ruler.

Now choose just two colors that you would like to use with the gold. You will see that most floral patterns on the letters are split into two, so you can use one color for each branch of pattern. For example, for the "*J*" I have used red and blue. Apply these colors in the same way as the gold. In order to define the letter and to give a uniform appearance we need to outline both the gold and the color. Introducing too many colors can make the work look messy. For the outline on the "*J*," I have added a tiny spot of blue to the vermilion tint. When you are outlining, it is helpful to keep the area being outlined on your left if you are right-handed, and vice versa if you are left-handed.

In order to emphasize the letter and to make it more ornate, you can now add some gold dots to the color and an outline of gold dots to the letter.

One tip to remember when outlining over paint is to make sure that the paint is bone dry and the outlining paint is not too runny. Paint always tends to spread slightly when applied on top of paint. The gold and color can be reversed, giving quite a different effect. Here are some further ideas to use:

1. *Trace down the letter.*
2. *Fill in all the gold areas.*
3. *Fill in all the colored areas.*
4. *Outline the letter, decoration and border.*
5. *Gold dots outlining the actual letter*
6. *Gold dots on the decoration*

This is designed as a birth announcement card. The first letter of the child's name, the date of birth (and/or christening or bris date can be included*) and the verse to go with the day of the child's birth.
*if used as a christening or invitation to a bris card.

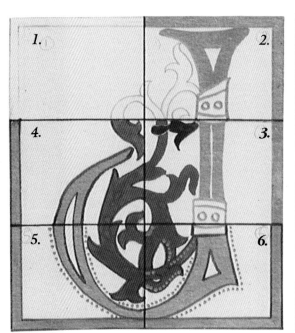

JANUARY ~ TUESDAYS

CHILD IS FULL OF GRACE

BORN TUESDAY NINETEENTH

KATIE JANE

C · H · A · P · T · E · R
· S · I · X ·

DECORATING A MOUNT

PROJECT 7

YOU WILL NEED TO GET a single or double mount cut by a picture framer in order to undertake this project. Mounts really do enhance your work and it is well worth doing this to anything on which you have spent time and effort.

DANIEL: For this name I cut a double mount, using a dark red underneath and ivory on top so it can be decorated. Start by measuring on equal distance all around from the inside bevelled edge of the mount. Add a further line and mark off several points at equal distances. All the straight lines are drawn with the mapping nib used against the bevelled edge of the ruler.

I have only used one color and gold to produce this name. The mountboard color and the color of the decoration on the mount reflect the colors in the name, giving a very rich effect.

STENCILING A BORDER

PROJECT 8

Y OU WILL NEED: · *a craft knife* · *thick card on which to cut out the stencil* · *a piece of ordinary sponge.*

Start by cutting out the stencil found in the back of the workstation, placing the card on a suitable surface on which to cut. Always pull the craft knife toward you when cutting. You will find that you need to turn the laminated card around constantly in order to cut efficiently.

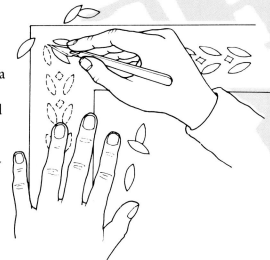

Next mix up some paint from the workstation on a saucer, making sure that the consistency is quite dry. Using a small piece of sponge about 1 inch x 2 inches square, dip into the paint. On a piece of rough paper, get rid of any excess paint and practice sponging the stencil.

The stencil can be placed either on the mount you have cut, or directly around the letter or poem on the card. You can introduce another color to give a two tone-effect.

There are some other border ideas on the stencil card at the back of the workstation.

These stenciled borders can be used for letters (instead of mounts), poems, greeting cards, bookmarks, etc.

Stencils are ideal for cards, it is a good way to mass produce your own cards without too much time and effort. The most time will be spent on cutting out the stencil.

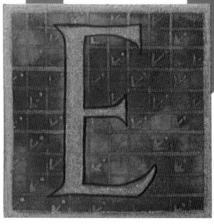

D: This D has been taken from the alphabet provided. The background is raised 23 ¼ carat gold leaf which has been indented with a burnisher.

Elizabeth the Second: This was designed as a heading for a Royal Warrant. The E is highly raised gesso with 23 ¼ carat gold leaf. The other gold letters are shell gold. The black text has been written using Chinese stick ink.

B: Again similar to the letters in project 8: raised 23 ¼ carat gold leaf for the letter and a bright blue background with gold paint on top. The decoration on the mount reflects the letter.

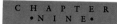

DECORATIVE VERSALS

PROJECT 10

T HE MODERN GOTHIC ALPHABET IS adapted from the Blackletter alphabet of the 15th century. It is easier to read than Blackletter and softer on the eyes! Combined with the decorative versals, some beautiful results can be attained.

The modern gothic written out with the pen, complements these fat, chunky Lombardic versals.

There are many styles of versals—from the plain modern types to the rather squat Lombardic versals of the 15th century, which were mainly used as decorative first letters in the old manuscript books.

modern gothic

abcdefghijkl

mnopqrs

tuvwxyz

1234567890

There are many ways you can use versals today, here are a few examples: greeting cards, invitations, Christmas cards, names on certificates and diplomas, wine labels, bookplates, logos, quotations, titles for poems, etc. Here are a few examples for you to copy. The versals can be traced and then outlined with paint using the mapping nib and then the paint flooded into the letter.

Brandy

C

Elderflower wine

H

GINGER WINE

Some of the versals are difficult to read (e.g. G in Ginger wine) and need simple letters to follow to make them readable.

Most dots and decoration are added after the main letter has been painted (happy birthday).

happy birthday

It is always a good idea to limit the amount of colors used. On these pages I have used no more than two colors and the effects are very striking.

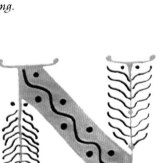

Keep the decoration fairly simple, do not let it make the design too busy.

Always pencil the letters out roughly, always calligraphy first (Pater noster) and then paint your fancy initial.

43

The tail of the Q must go down far enough so as not to interfere with the next letter when used in a word.

Rue

Savory

To save space in the word wood, the letters have been evenly overlapped.

Wormwood

Yarrow

BORDER, FILLERS & PICTURES

PROJECT 11

HERE ARE SOME IDEAS FOR decorating your work. Some can be used as borders, some as corner decorations, and some can be used inside initials, etc.

A nice effect of thick and thin lines can be achieved with the calligraphy nib and mapping pen. When using the calligraphy nib to actually produce an illustration—for example, the flowers, hearts or the bird—an interesting effect is produced by the way the nib becomes thick and thin. This result is produced by keeping the nib the same angle (approximately 30–40 degrees) as you would when writing some letters, this effect particularly shows up when using gold.

It is always a good idea to draw yourself some guidelines.

This will keep your decorations more even and give you more confidence.

Pictures are a great idea for letter headings, can be used as line fillers (if a line of a poem is too short), and inside large initials as decorations.

*Once you get the hang of the borders, they can be quite quick
to do and are ideal for cards, etc.*

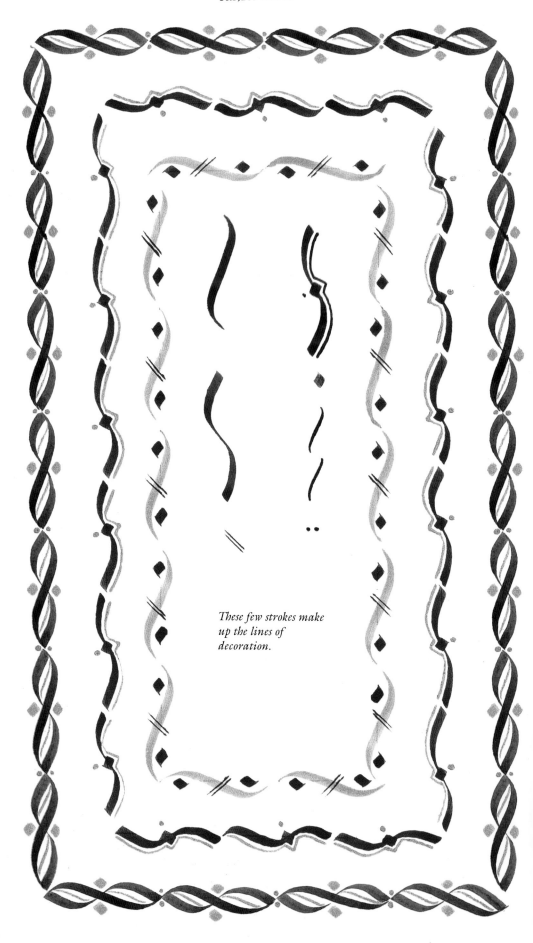

These few strokes make
up the lines of
decoration.

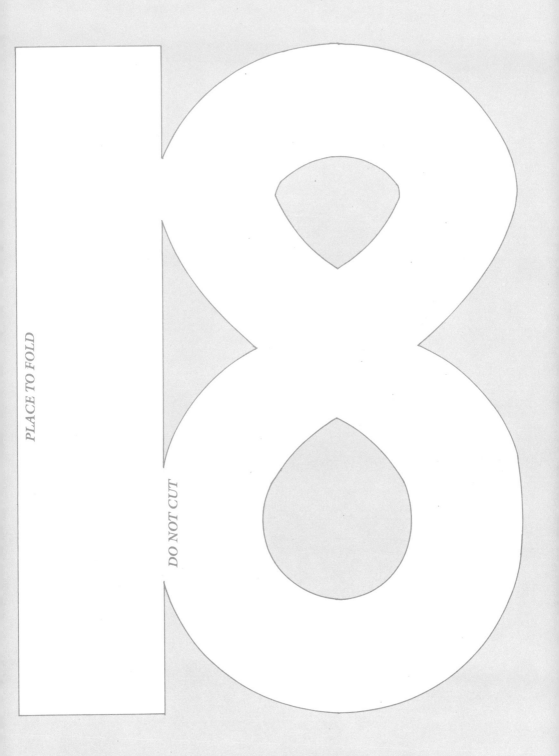

PLACE TO FOLD

DO NOT CUT

CUT OUT SHADED AREAS

PLACE TO FOLD

PLACE TO FOLD

DO NOT CUT

CUT OUT SHADED AREAS

STENCIL

Tear out this sheet and glue to a
sheet of stiff card before cutting
out the stencils.

OTHER IDEAS FOR STENCILS

CUT OUT SHADED AREAS

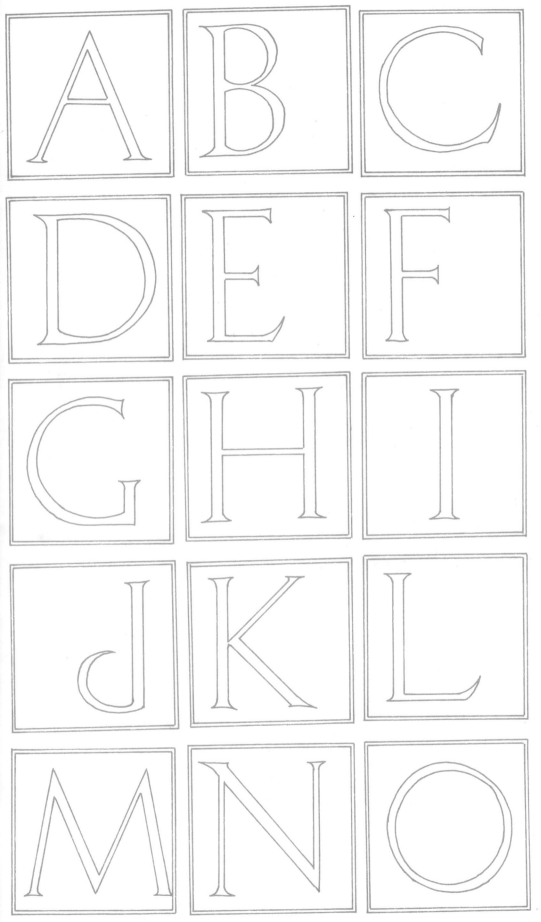

*ADD THIS TAIL TO THE O
TO MAKE Q*

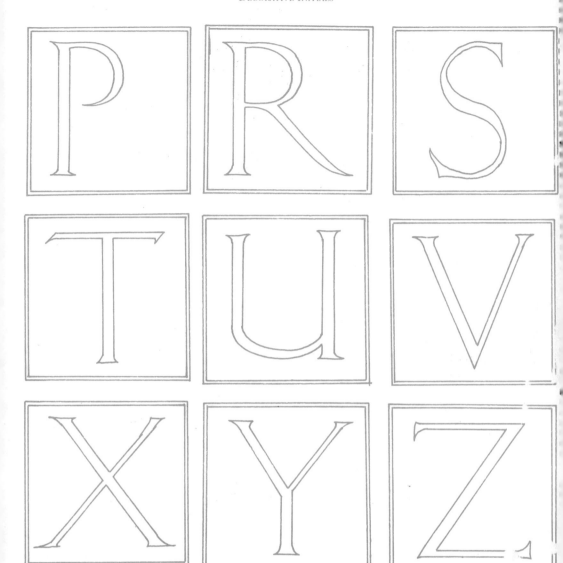